Dear Parents:

Congratulations! Your child is taking the first steps on an exciting journey. The destination? Independent reading!

STEP INTO READING® will help your child get there. The program offers five steps to reading success. Each step includes fun stories and colorful art or photographs. In addition to original fiction and books with favorite characters, there are Step into Reading Non-Fiction Readers, Phonics Readers and Boxed Sets, Sticker Readers, and Comic Readers—a complete literacy program with something to interest every child.

Learning to Read, Step by Step!

Ready to Read Preschool–Kindergarten
• big type and easy words • rhyme and rhythm • picture clues
For children who know the alphabet and are eager to begin reading.

Reading with Help Preschool–Grade 1
• basic vocabulary • short sentences • simple stories
For children who recognize familiar words and sound out new words with help.

Reading on Your Own Grades 1–3
• engaging characters • easy-to-follow plots • popular topics
For children who are ready to read on their own.

Reading Paragraphs Grades 2–3
• challenging vocabulary • short paragraphs • exciting stories
For newly independent readers who read simple sentences with confidence.

Ready for Chapters Grades 2–4
• chapters • longer paragraphs • full-color art
For children who want to take the plunge into chapter books but still like colorful pictures.

STEP INTO READING® is designed to give every child a successful reading experience. The grade levels are only guides; children will progress through the steps at their own speed, developing confidence in their reading.

Remember, a lifetime love of reading starts with a single step!

Visit us on the Web!
StepIntoReading.com
rhcbooks.com

ISBN 978-0-593-12806-0 (trade) — ISBN 978-0-593-12807-7 (lib. bdg.)

Printed in the United States of America

10 9 8 7 6 5 4 3 2 1

Random House supports the First Amendment and celebrates the right to read.

Sunny Day™

BUSY BUNNY

by Tex Huntley

based on the teleplay "Violet's Adventure"
by Jodi Reynolds

illustrated by Susan Hall

Random House 🏠 New York

Rox loves Violet.

Violet is her bunny.

Sunny gives Rox
a bunny hairdo.

Rox is ready to skate.

But Violet sits

on the skateboard.

She rolls out the door!

Sunny, Rox, and Blair
run to the Glam Van.

They look for Violet.

Violet hops onto Peter's flower cart.

The cart rolls
down the street!

Violet hops
into Lacey's
flower basket.

Rox gets her
skateboard back.
Violet hops away again.

Violet is on
a Ferris wheel!

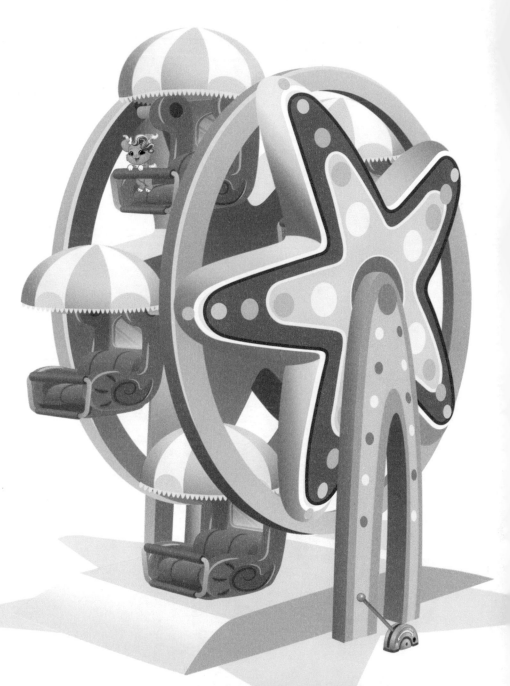

Sunny and Lacey try
to stop the wheel.
It gets stuck!

Rox climbs up, up, up.

Rox saves Violet!

Can they get down?

Rox pulls a ribbon
from her hairdo.
She tows the
skateboard up.

Rox and Violet
slide down
the ribbon.

Violet is safe!
The busy day
is over.

Sunny, Blair, and Rox
all love Violet!